Gertrude Chandler Warner's

THE BOXCAR CHILDREN GRAPHIC NOVELS

BOOK NINE
THE HAUNTED CABIN MYSTERY

Henry, Jessie, Violet, and Benny take a trip down the Mississippi River in a paddle-wheel boat and stay in a haunted cabin! At least it seems haunted—there are spooky phone calls, flickering lights, and strange shadows. Are there really ghosts, or is someone trying to scare the Boxcar Children away?

THE BOXCAR CHILDREN
GRAPHIC NOVELS

1. THE BOXCAR CHILDREN
2. SURPRISE ISLAND
3. THE YELLOW HOUSE MYSTERY
4. MYSTERY RANCH
5. MIKE'S MYSTERY
6. BLUE BAY MYSTERY
7. SNOWBOUND MYSTERY
8. TREE HOUSE MYSTERY
9. THE HAUNTED CABIN MYSTERY
10. THE AMUSEMENT PARK MYSTERY
11. THE PIZZA MYSTERY
12. THE CASTLE MYSTERY

Gertrude Chandler Warner's

THE BOXCAR CHILDREN
THE HAUNTED CABIN MYSTERY

Adapted by Jeff Limke
Illustrated by Mark Bloodworth

Henry Alden

Watch

Jessie Alden

Violet Alden

Benny Alden

magic
wagon

Visit us at www.abdopublishing.com

Published by Magic Wagon, a division of the ABDO Group, 8000 West 78th Street, Edina, Minnesota 55439.

Printed in the United States of America, North Mankato, Minnesota
092009
012010
Printed On Recycled Paper.

Adapted by Jeff Limke
Illustrated by Mark Bloodworth
Colored by Carlos Badilla
Lettered by Johnny Lowe
Interior layout and design by Kristen Fitzner Denton
Cover art by Mike Dubisch
Book design and packaging by Shannon Eric Denton

Library of Congress Cataloging-in-Publication Data

Limke, Jeff.
The haunted cabin mystery / adapted by Jeff Limke ; illustrated by Mark Bloodworth.
p. cm. -- (The Boxcar Children graphic novels)
"Gertrude Chandler Warner's The Boxcar Children."
Summary: The Alden children travel on a Mississippi paddle-wheel steamer to visit an old family friend in his cabin near Hannibal, Missouri, and try to discover who is responsible for the mysterious activities near the house.
ISBN 978-1-60270-717-7
1. Graphic novels. [1. Graphic novels. 2. Brothers and sisters--Fiction. 3. Orphans--Fiction. 4. Mississippi River--Fiction. 5. Buried treasure--Fiction. 6. Mystery and detective stories.] I. Bloodworth, Mark, ill. II. Warner, Gertrude Chandler, 1890-1979. Haunted cabin mystery. III. Title.
PZ7.7.L55Hau 2010
741.5'973--dc22

2009029345

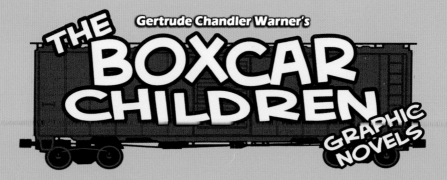

Gertrude Chandler Warner's

THE BOXCAR CHILDREN GRAPHIC NOVELS

BOOK NINE

THE HAUNTED CABIN MYSTERY

Contents

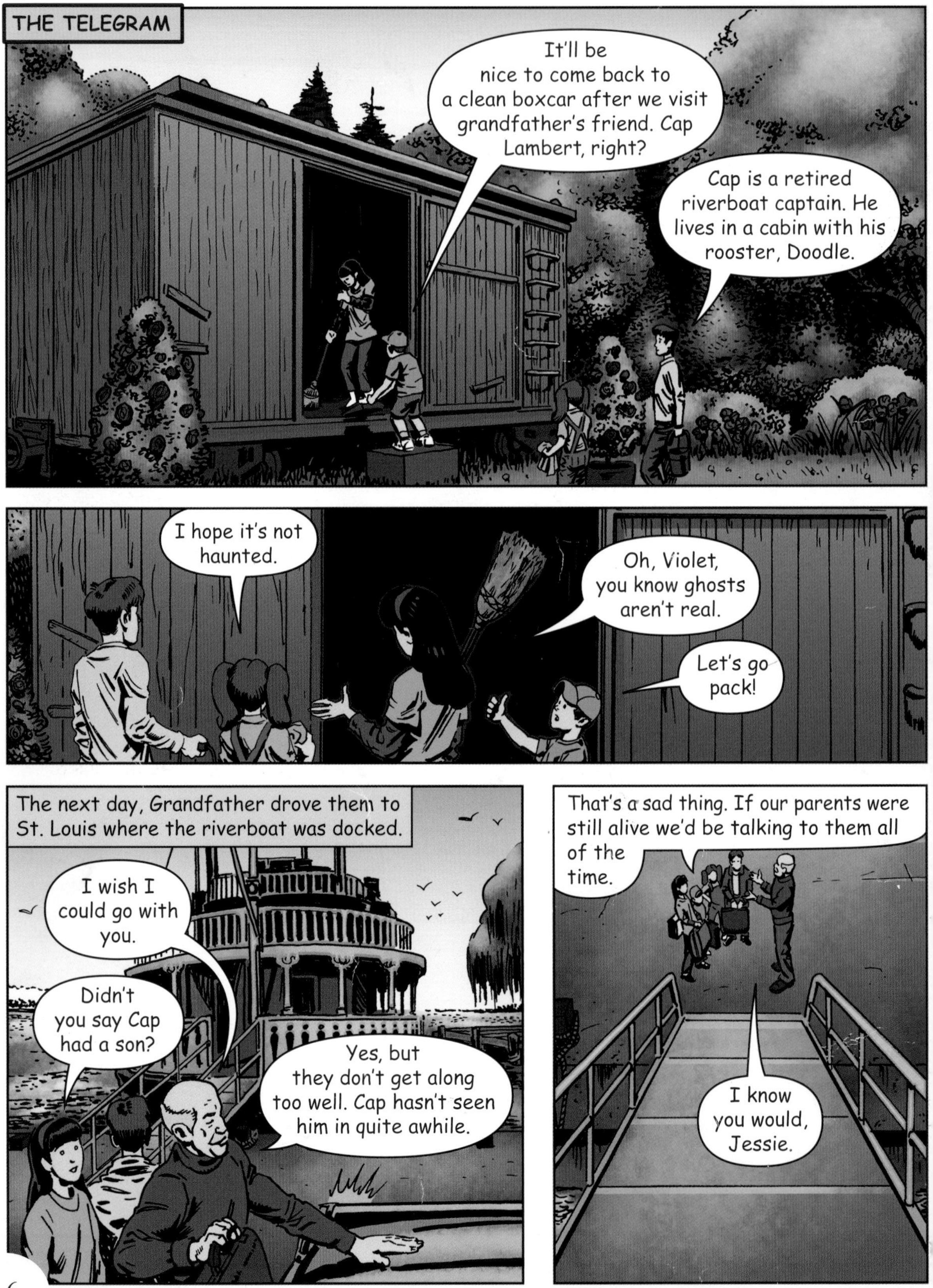
THE TELEGRAM
It'll be nice to come back to a clean boxcar after we visit grandfather's friend. Cap Lambert, right?
Cap is a retired riverboat captain. He lives in a cabin with his rooster, Doodle.
I hope it's not haunted.
Oh, Violet, you know ghosts aren't real.
Let's go pack!
The next day, Grandfather drove them to St. Louis where the riverboat was docked.
I wish I could go with you.
Didn't you say Cap had a son?
Yes, but they don't get along too well. Cap hasn't seen him in quite awhile.
That's a sad thing. If our parents were still alive we'd be talking to them all of the time.
I know you would, Jessie.

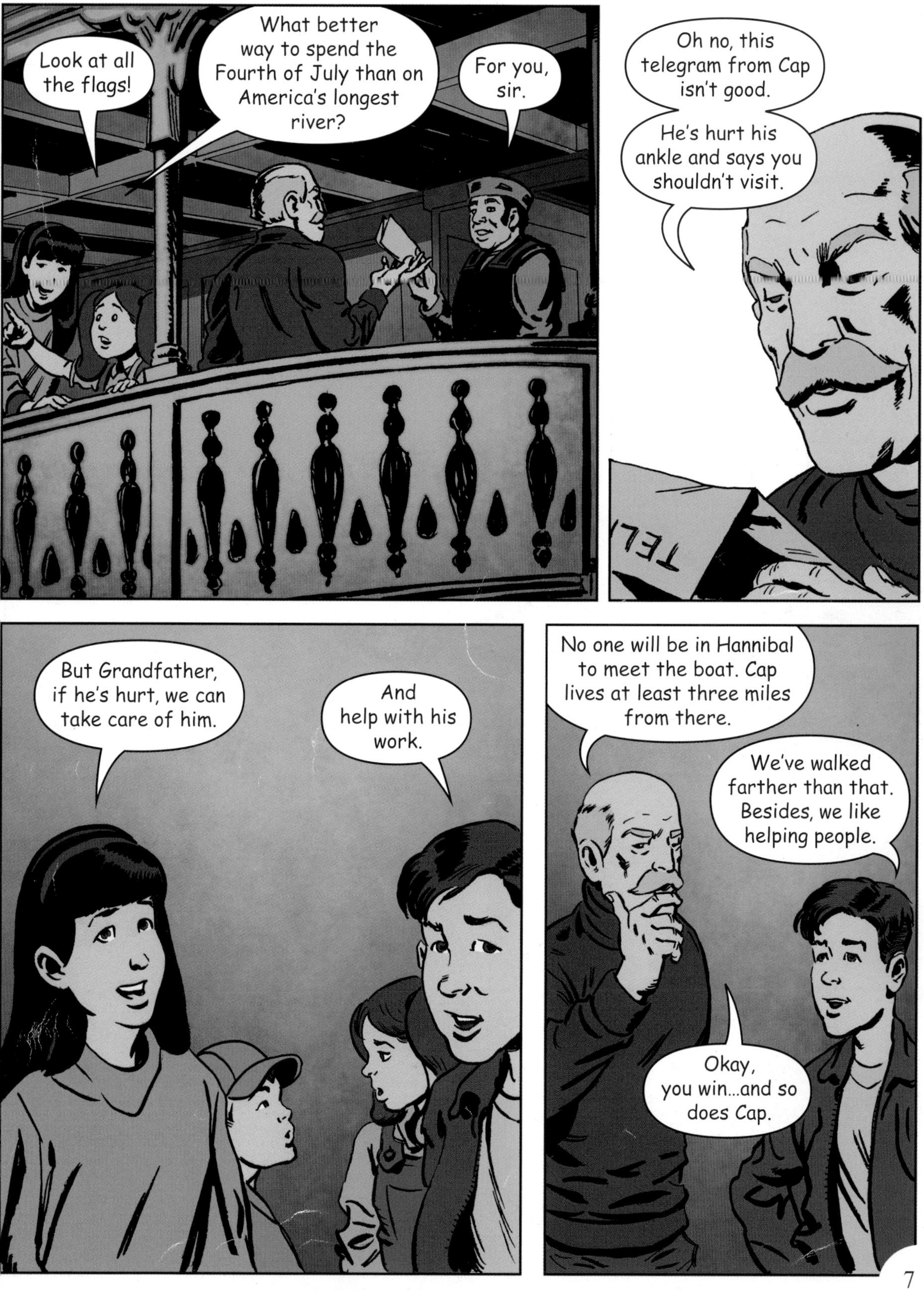
Look at all the flags!
What better way to spend the Fourth of July than on America's longest river?
For you, sir.
Oh no, this telegram from Cap isn't good.
He's hurt his ankle and says you shouldn't visit.
But Grandfather, if he's hurt, we can take care of him.
And help with his work.
No one will be in Hannibal to meet the boat. Cap lives at least three miles from there.
We've walked farther than that. Besides, we like helping people.
Okay, you win...and so does Cap.

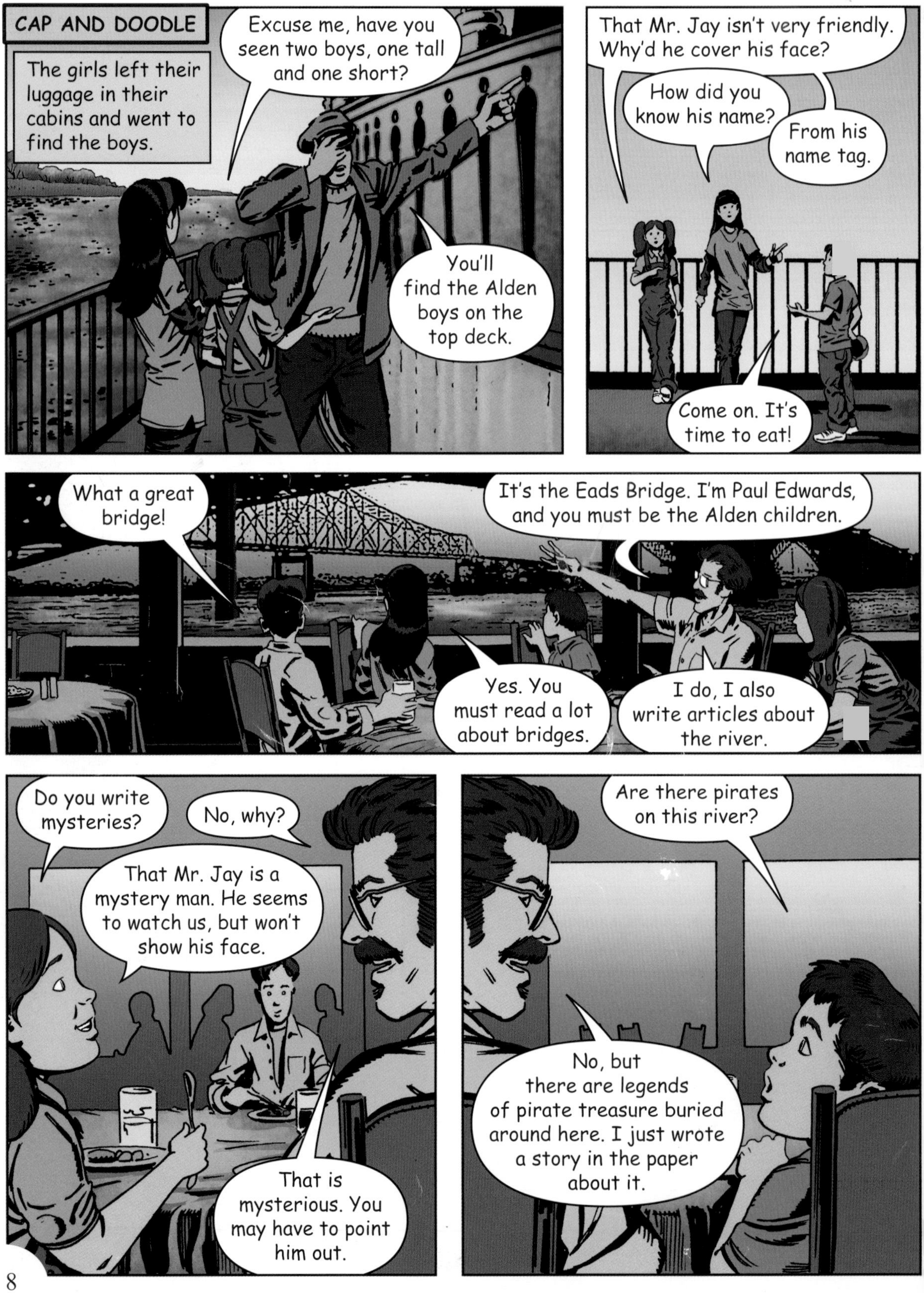
CAP AND DOODLE
The girls left their luggage in their cabins and went to find the boys.
Excuse me, have you seen two boys, one tall and one short?
You'll find the Alden boys on the top deck.
That Mr. Jay isn't very friendly. Why'd he cover his face?
How did you know his name?
From his name tag.
Come on. It's time to eat!
What a great bridge!
It's the Eads Bridge. I'm Paul Edwards, and you must be the Alden children.
Yes. You must read a lot about bridges.
I do, I also write articles about the river.
Do you write mysteries?
No, why?
That Mr. Jay is a mystery man. He seems to watch us, but won't show his face.
That is mysterious. You may have to point him out.
Are there pirates on this river?
No, but there are legends of pirate treasure buried around here. I just wrote a story in the paper about it.

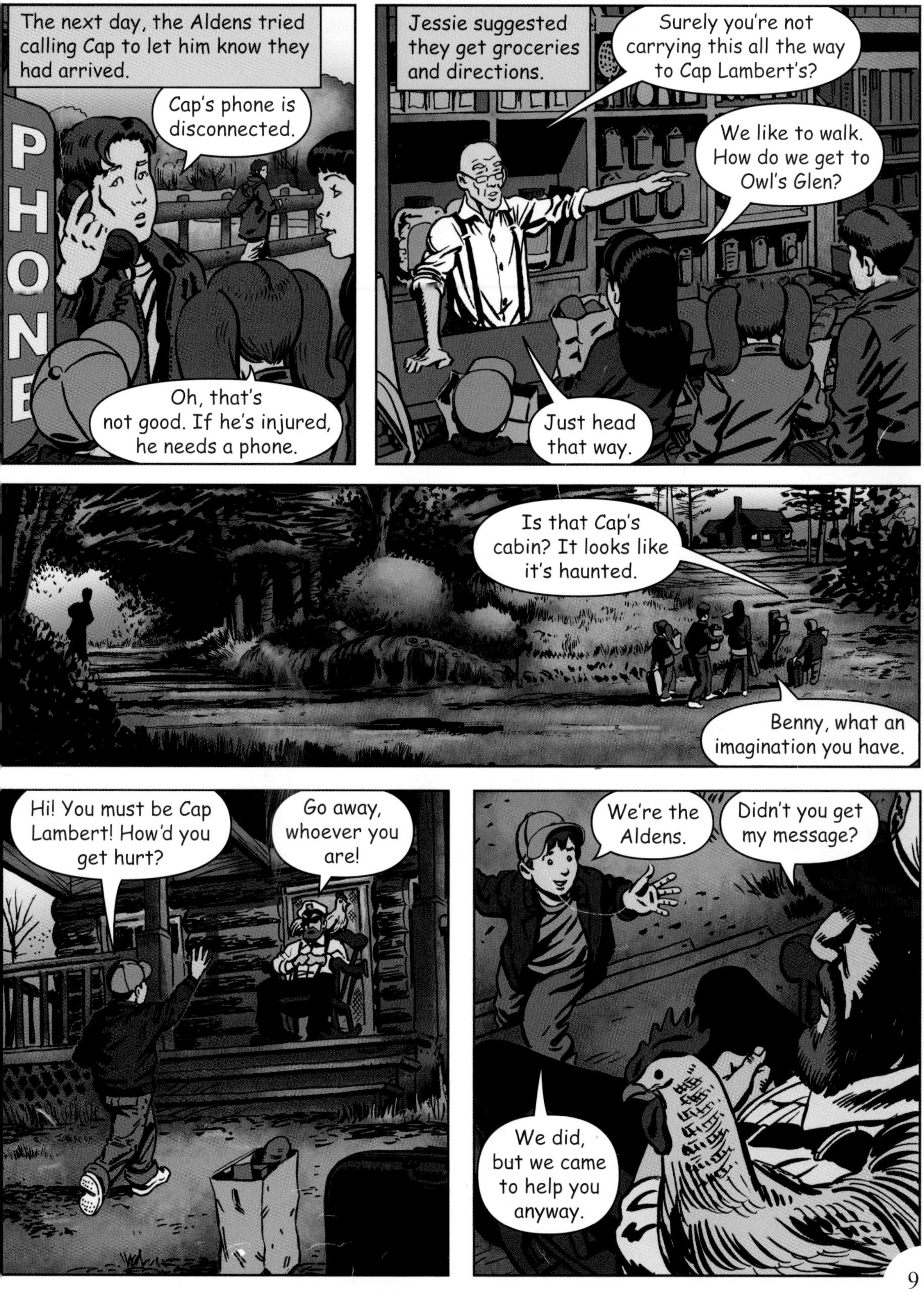

The next day, the Aldens tried calling Cap to let him know they had arrived.
PHONE
Cap's phone is disconnected.
Oh, that's not good. If he's injured, he needs a phone.
Jessie suggested they get groceries and directions.
Surely you're not carrying this all the way to Cap Lambert's?
We like to walk. How do we get to Owl's Glen?
Just head that way.
Is that Cap's cabin? It looks like it's haunted.
Benny, what an imagination you have.
Hi! You must be Cap Lambert! How'd you get hurt?
Go away, whoever you are!
We're the Aldens.
Didn't you get my message?
We did, but we came to help you anyway.

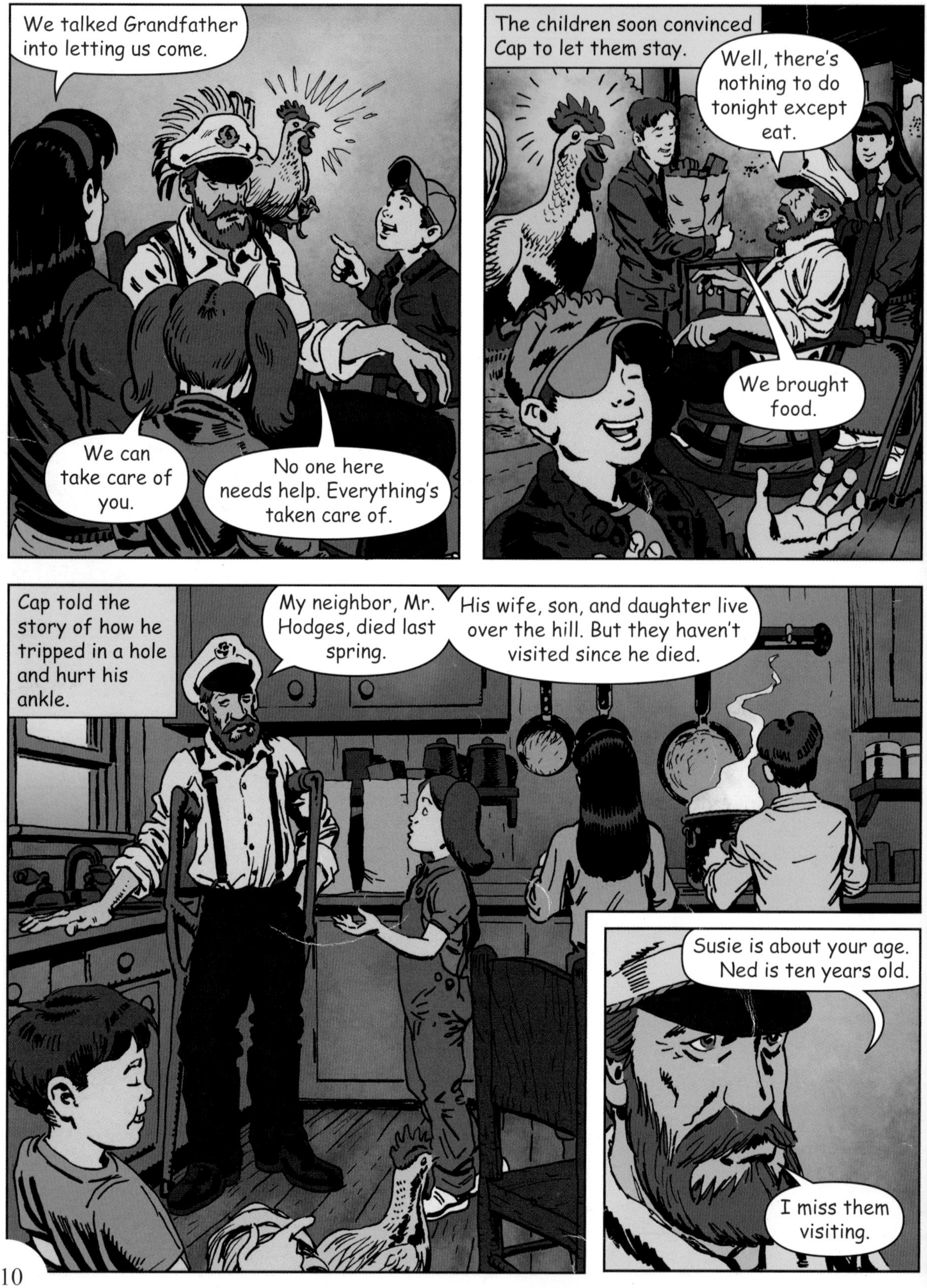

We talked Grandfather into letting us come.
We can take care of you.
No one here needs help. Everything's taken care of.
The children soon convinced Cap to let them stay.
We brought food.
Well, there's nothing to do tonight except eat.
Cap told the story of how he tripped in a hole and hurt his ankle.
My neighbor, Mr. Hodges, died last spring.
His wife, son, and daughter live over the hill. But they haven't visited since he died.
Susie is about your age. Ned is ten years old.
I miss them visiting.

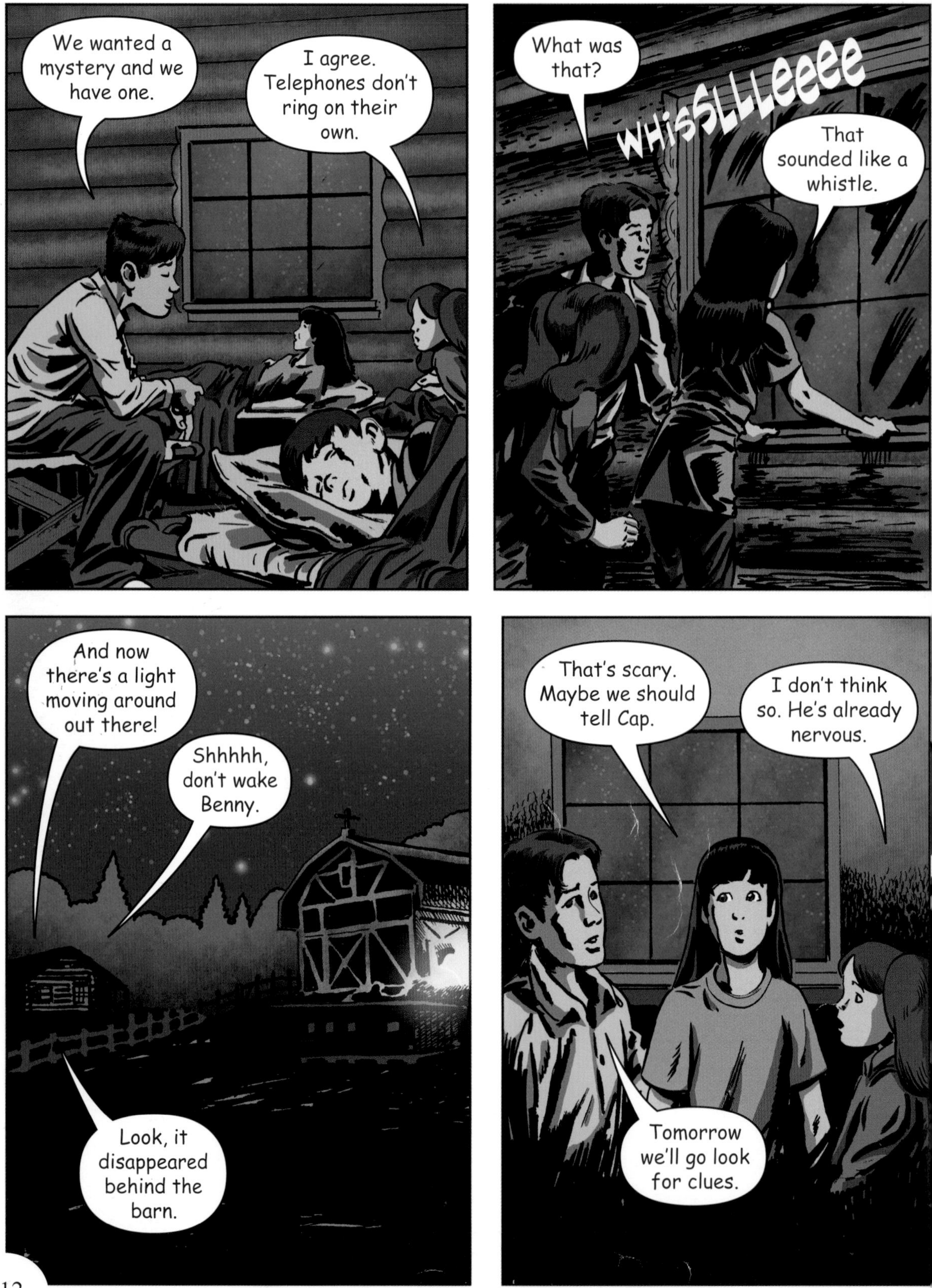
We wanted a mystery and we have one.
I agree. Telephones don't ring on their own.
What was that?
WHISSLLLEEEE
That sounded like a whistle.
And now there's a light moving around out there!
Shhhhh, don't wake Benny.
Look, it disappeared behind the barn.
That's scary. Maybe we should tell Cap.
I don't think so. He's already nervous.
Tomorrow we'll go look for clues.

14

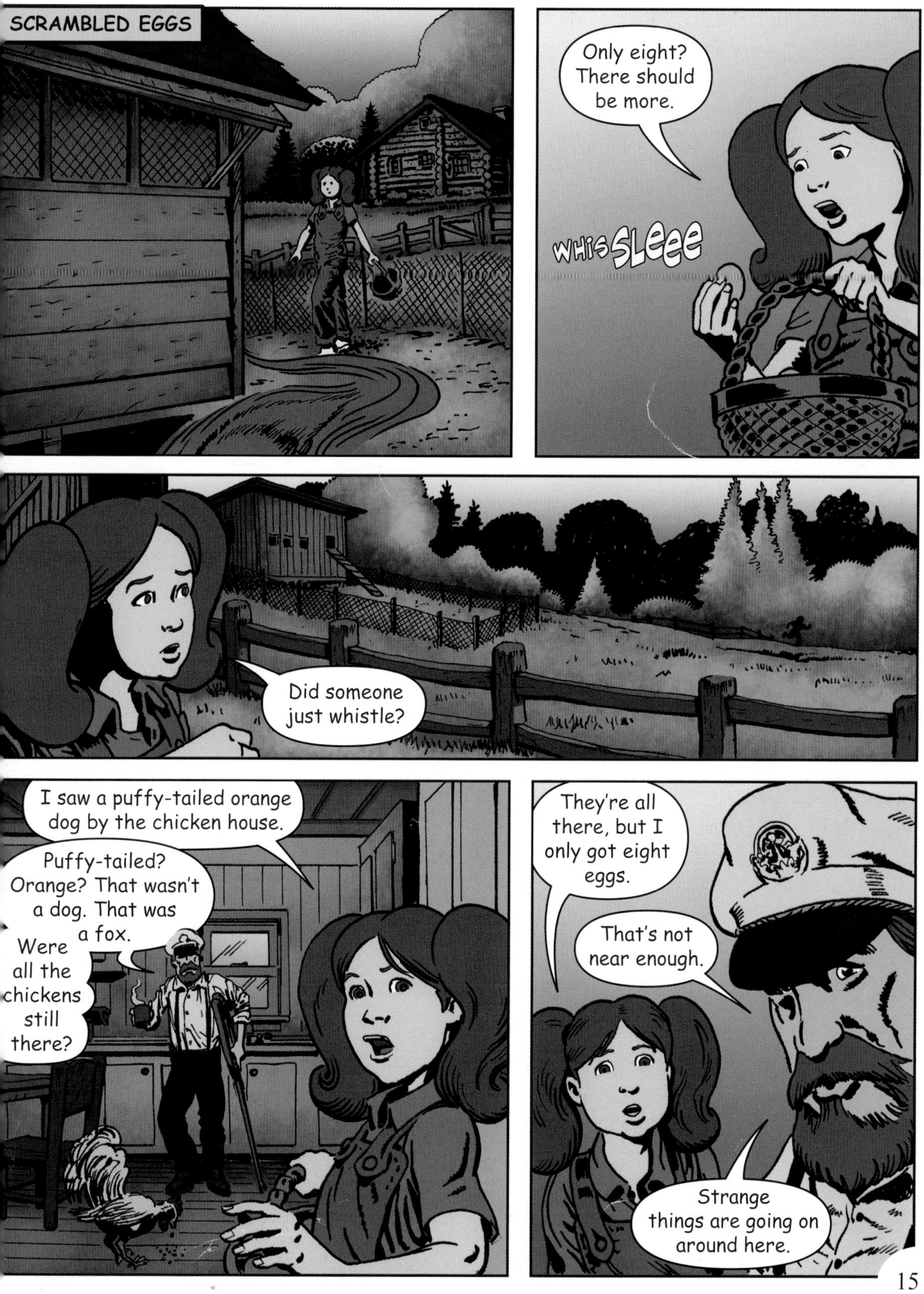
SCRAMBLED EGGS
Only eight? There should be more.
WHISSLEEE
Did someone just whistle?
I saw a puffy-tailed orange dog by the chicken house.
Puffy-tailed? Orange? That wasn't a dog. That was a fox.
Were all the chickens still there?
They're all there, but I only got eight eggs.
That's not near enough.
Strange things are going on around here.

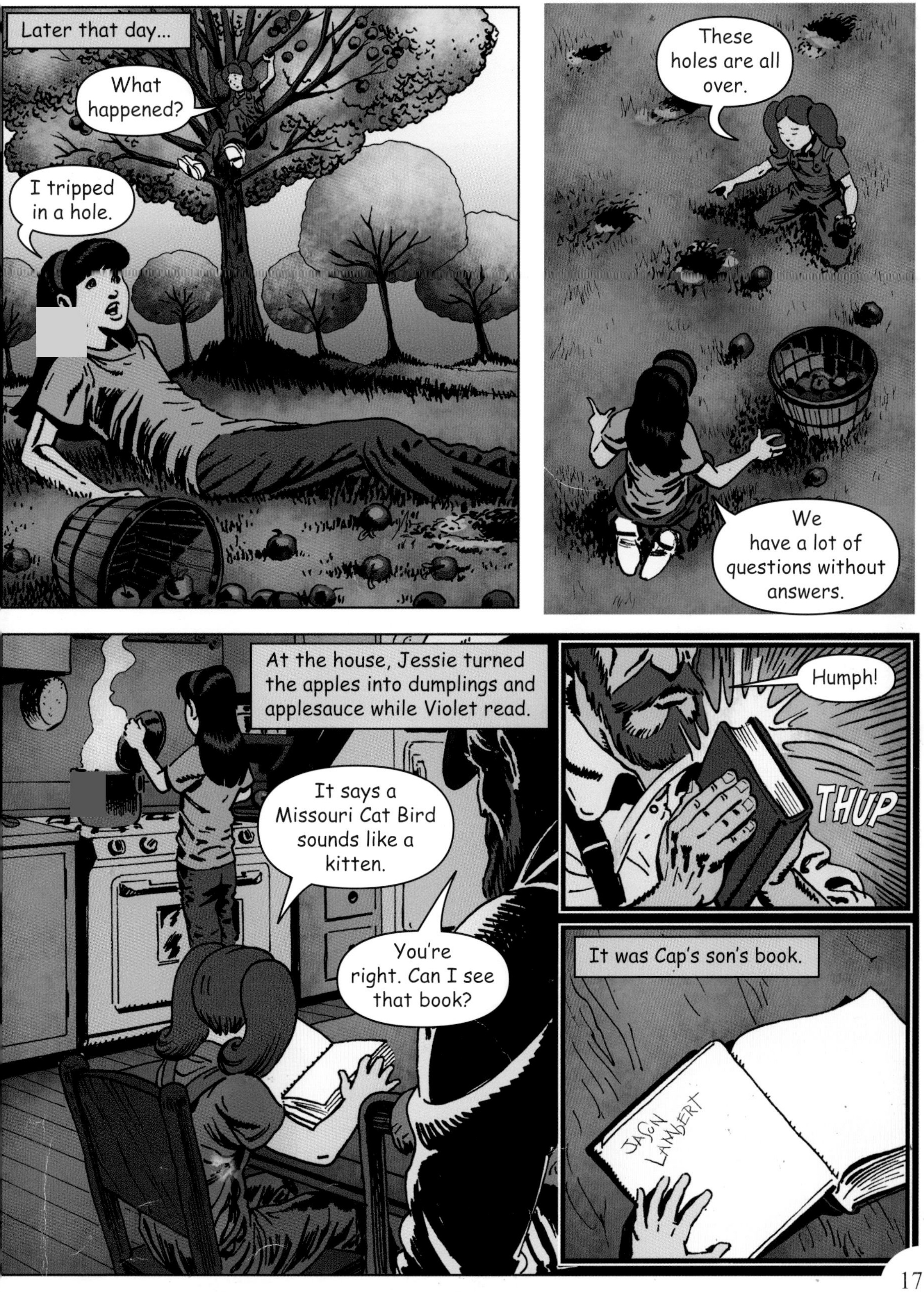
Later that day...
What happened?
I tripped in a hole.
These holes are all over.
We have a lot of questions without answers.
At the house, Jessie turned the apples into dumplings and applesauce while Violet read.
It says a Missouri Cat Bird sounds like a kitten.
You're right. Can I see that book?
Humph!
THUP
It was Cap's son's book.
JASON LAMBERT

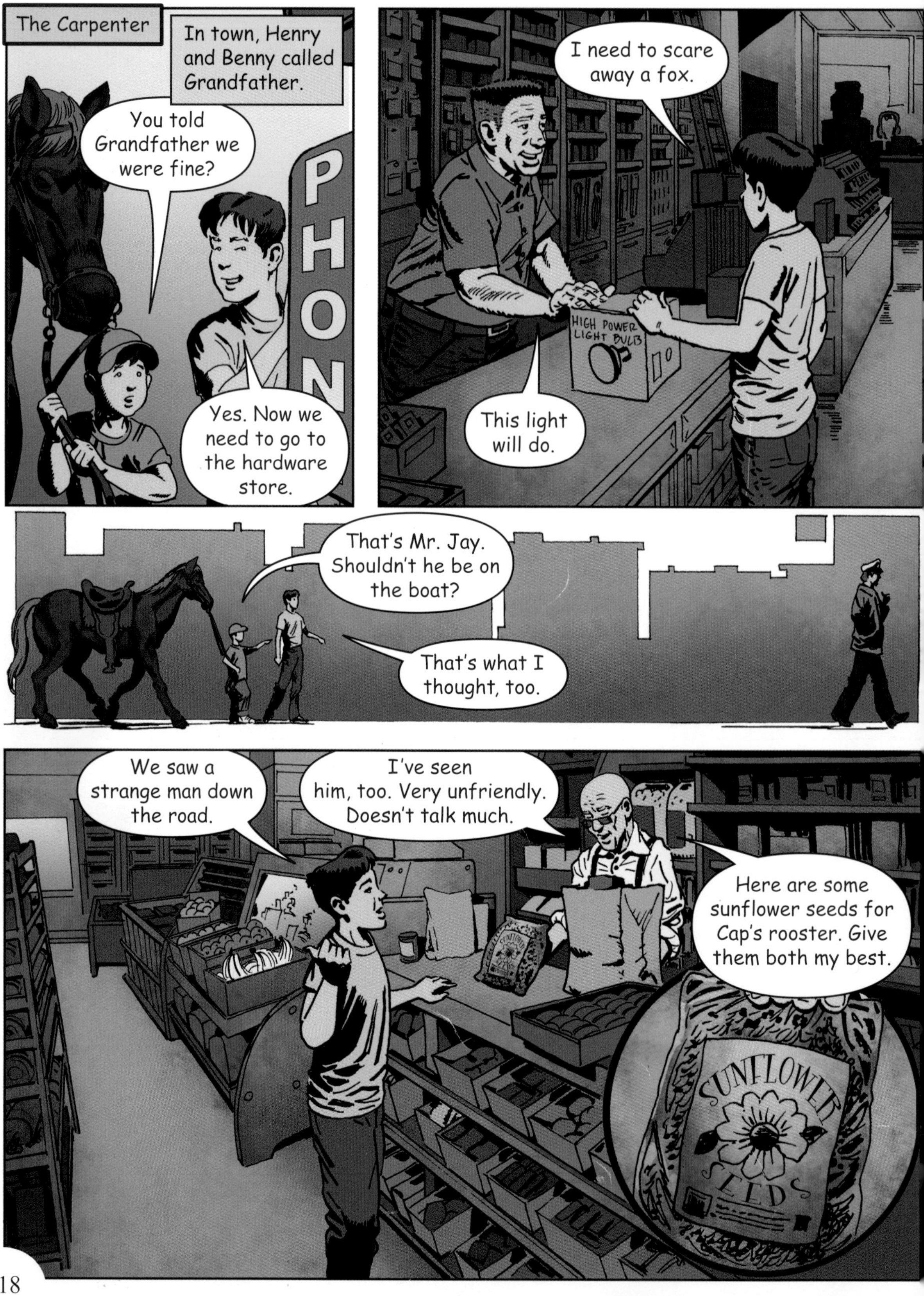

The Carpenter
In town, Henry and Benny called Grandfather.
You told Grandfather we were fine?
Yes. Now we need to go to the hardware store.
PHON
I need to scare away a fox.
This light will do.
HIGH POWER LIGHT BULB
That's Mr. Jay. Shouldn't he be on the boat?
That's what I thought, too.
We saw a strange man down the road.
I've seen him, too. Very unfriendly. Doesn't talk much.
Here are some sunflower seeds for Cap's rooster. Give them both my best.
SUNFLOWER SEEDS

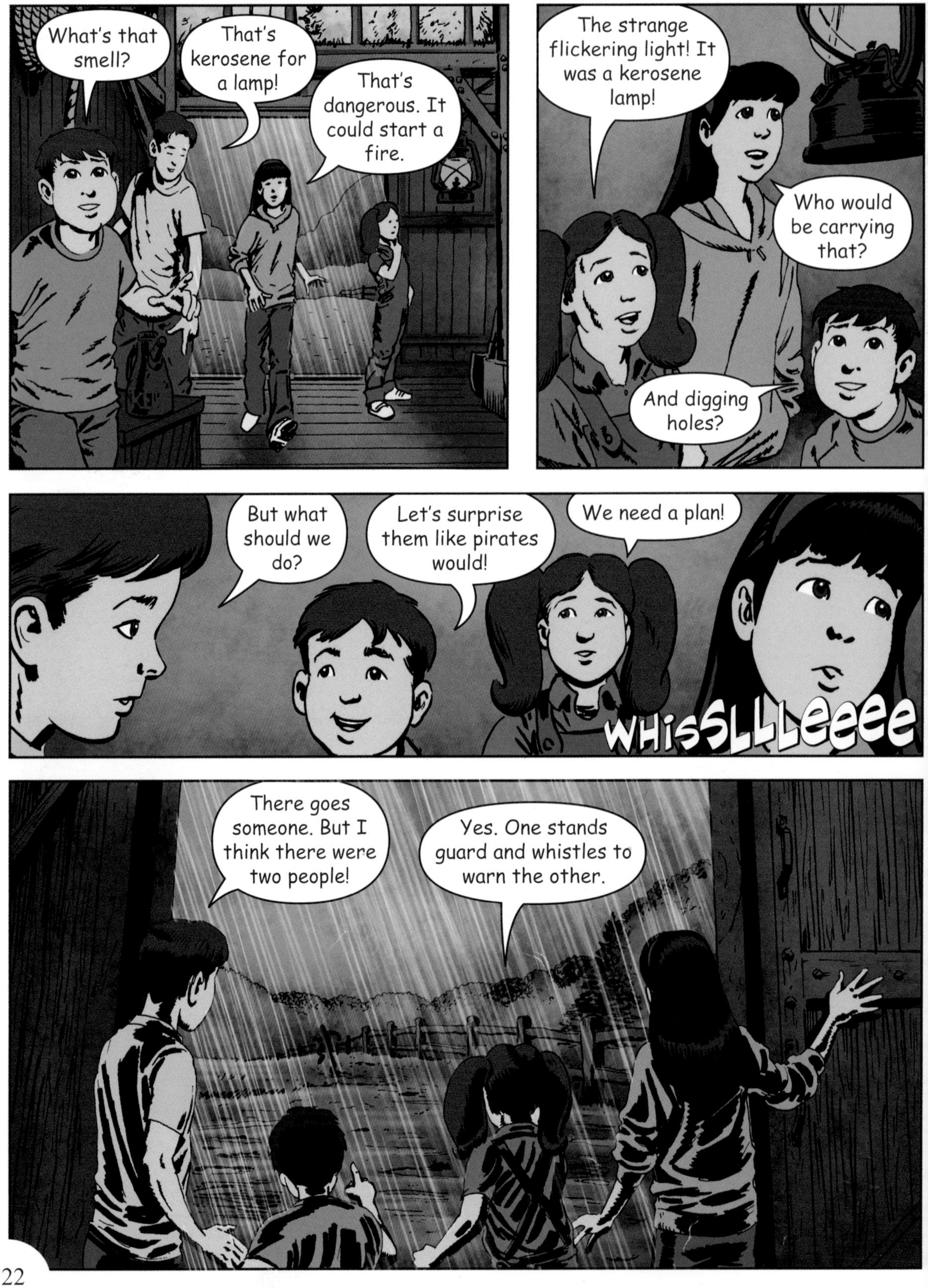
What's that smell?
That's kerosene for a lamp!
That's dangerous. It could start a fire.
The strange flickering light! It was a kerosene lamp!
Who would be carrying that?
And digging holes?
But what should we do?
Let's surprise them like pirates would!
We need a plan!
WHISSLLLEEEE
There goes someone. But I think there were two people!
Yes. One stands guard and whistles to warn the other.

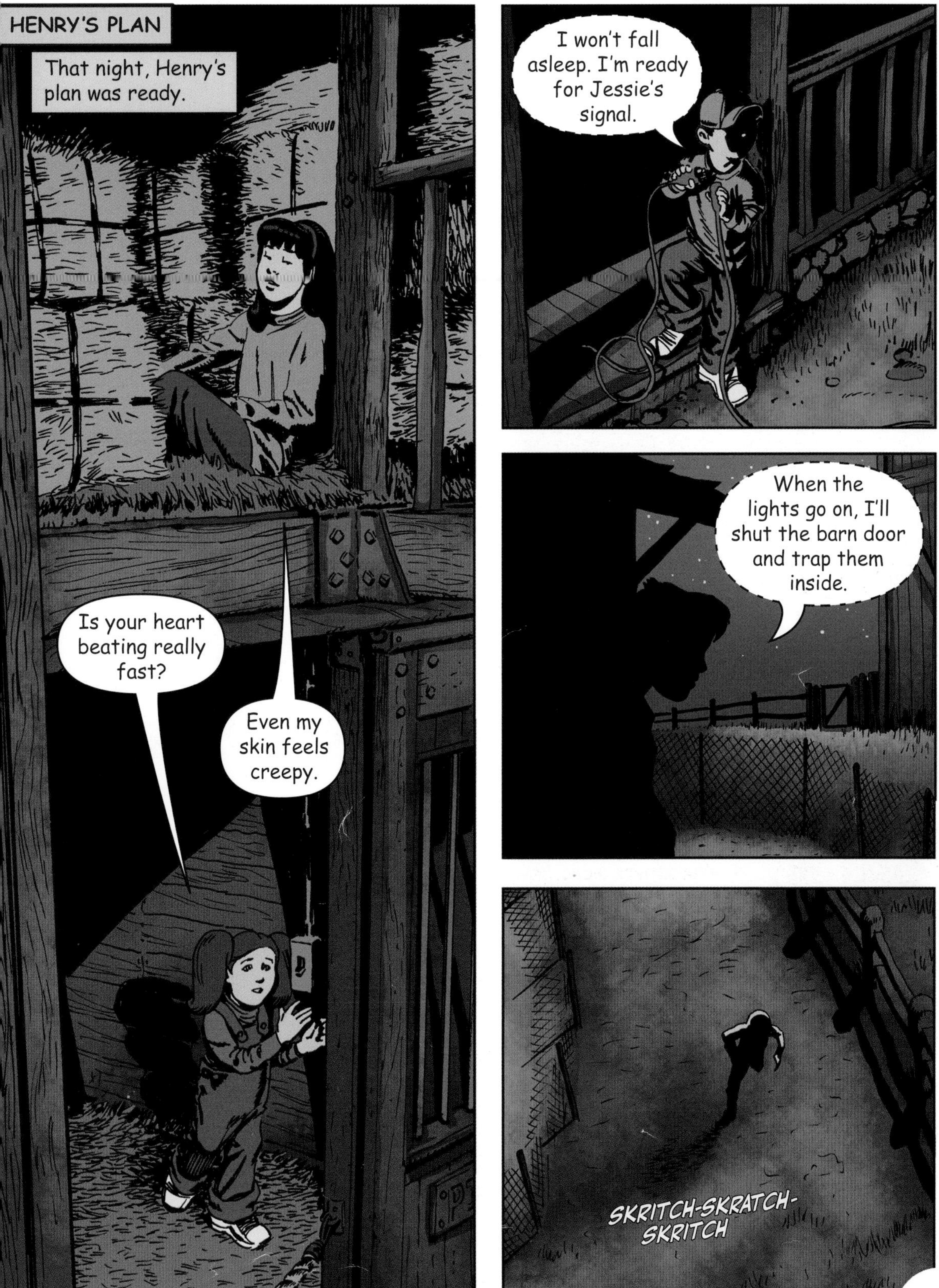
HENRY'S PLAN
That night, Henry's plan was ready.
Is your heart beating really fast?
Even my skin feels creepy.
I won't fall asleep. I'm ready for Jessie's signal.
When the lights go on, I'll shut the barn door and trap them inside.
SKRITCH-SKRATCH-SKRITCH

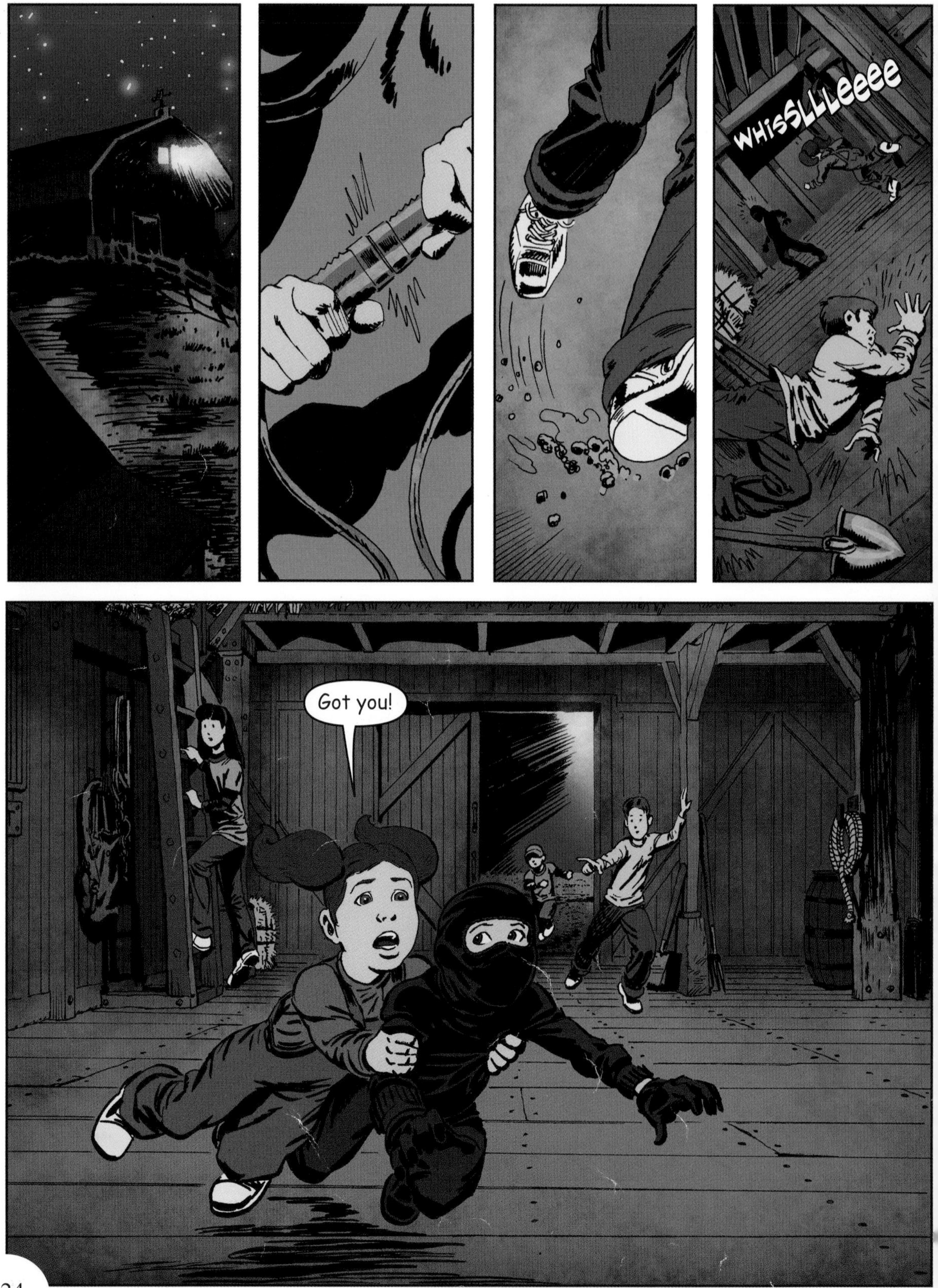
WHISSLLLEEEE
Got you!

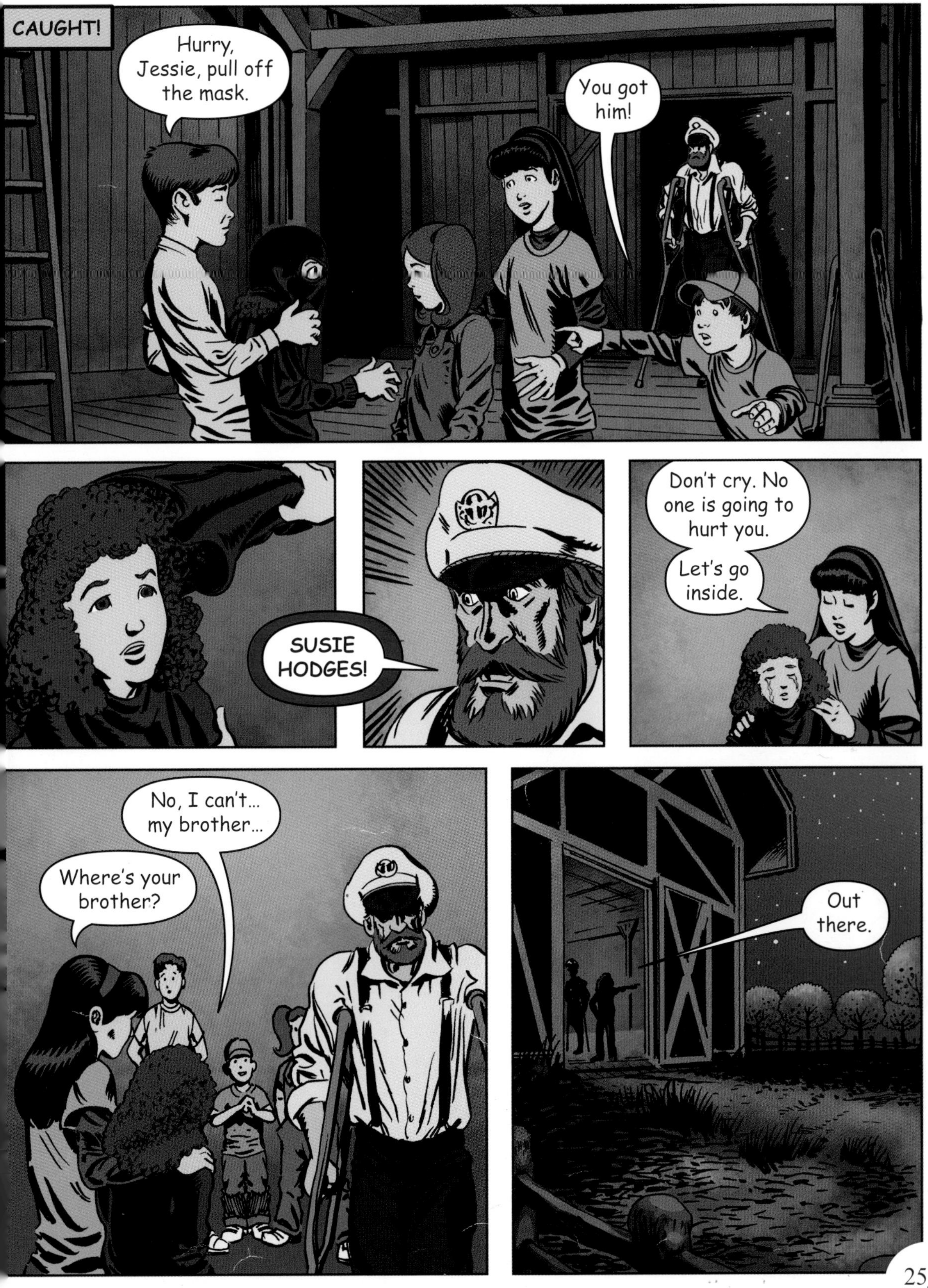
CAUGHT!
Hurry, Jessie, pull off the mask.
You got him!
SUSIE HODGES!
Don't cry. No one is going to hurt you.
Let's go inside.
No, I can't... my brother...
Where's your brother?
Out there.

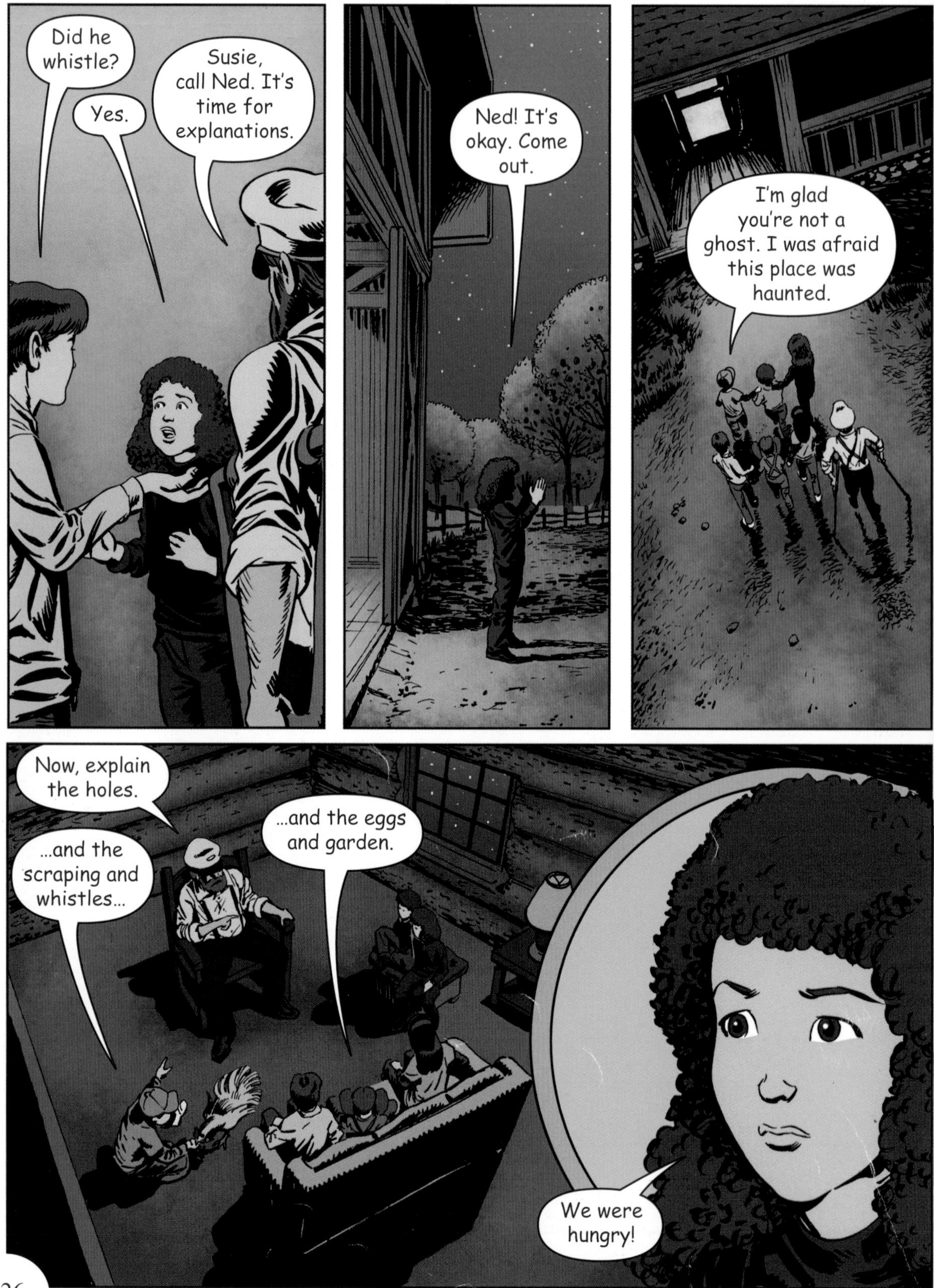
Did he whistle?
Yes.
Susie, call Ned. It's time for explanations.
Ned! It's okay. Come out.
I'm glad you're not a ghost. I was afraid this place was haunted.
Now, explain the holes.
...and the scraping and whistles...
...and the eggs and garden.
We were hungry!

THE REAL TREASURE

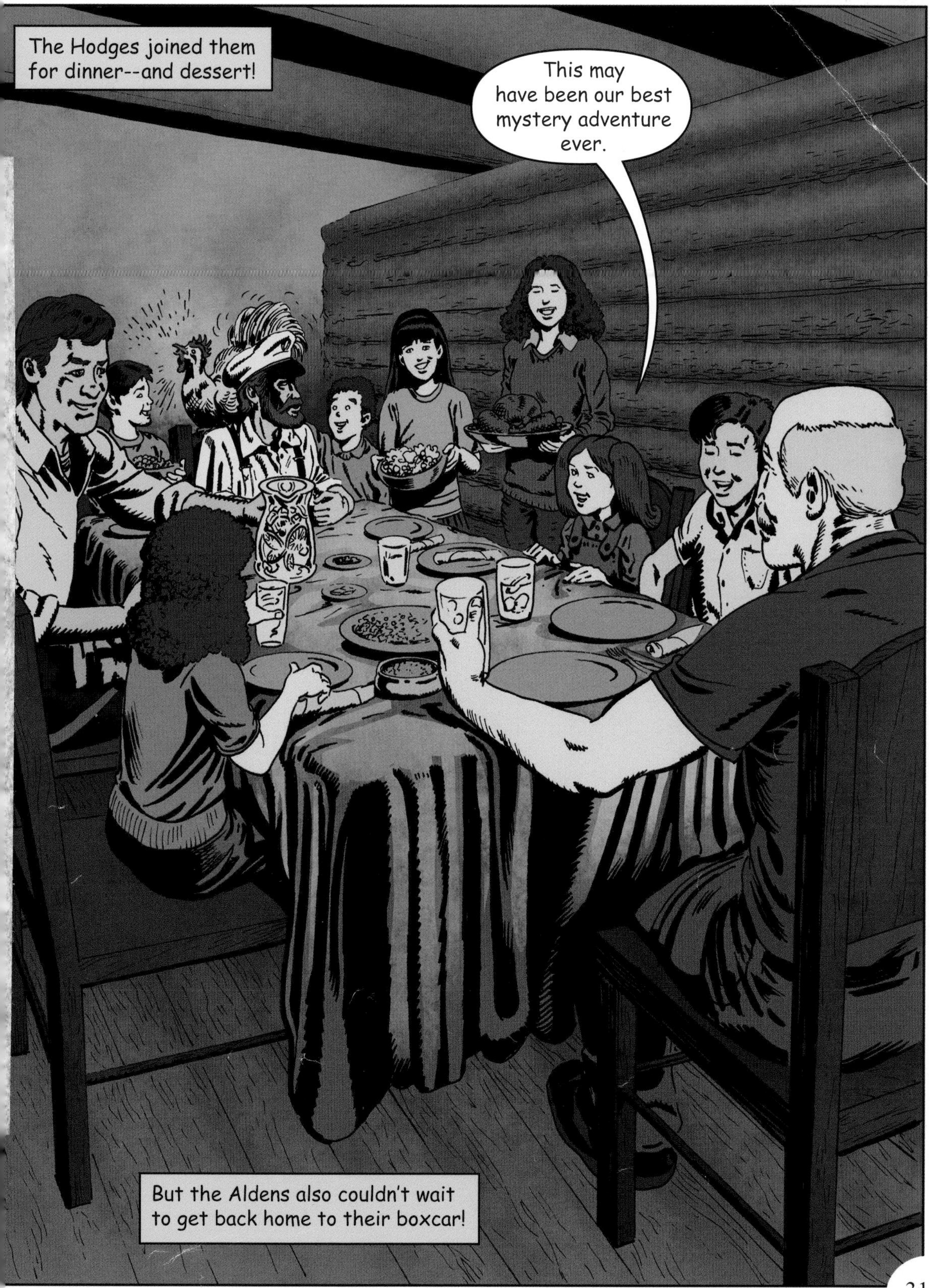
The Hodges joined them for dinner--and dessert!
This may have been our best mystery adventure ever.
But the Aldens also couldn't wait to get back home to their boxcar!

ABOUT THE CREATOR

Gertrude Chandler Warner was born on April 16, 1890, in Putnam, Connecticut. In 1918, Warner began teaching at Israel Putnam School. As a teacher, she discovered that many readers who liked an exciting story could not find books that were both easy and fun to read. She decided to try to meet this need. In 1942, *The Boxcar Children* was published for these readers.

Warner drew on her own experience to write *The Boxcar Children*. As a child she spent hours watching trains go by on the tracks near her family home. She often dreamed about what it would be like to live in a caboose or freight car—just as the Alden children do.

When readers asked for more Alden adventures, Warner began additional stories. While the mystery element is central to each of the books, she never thought of them as strictly juvenile mysteries. She liked to stress the Aldens' independence. Henry, Jessie, Violet, and Benny go about most of their adventures with as little adult supervision as possible—something that delights young readers.

During her lifetime, Warner received hundreds of letters from fans as she continued the Aldens' adventures, writing nineteen Boxcar Children books in all. After her death in 1979, her publisher, Albert Whitman and Company, carried on Warner's vision. Today, the Boxcar Children series has more than 100 books.